GRIEF & *Sunshine*

Written by

AYUSHI

INKTHOUGHT
PRESS

INKTHOUGHT
PRESS

Made with ❤ INKTHOUGHT PRESS

CHAPTERS

GRIEF: UNSPOKEN LOVE

What is love? What do we truly understand when we hear the word love?

When I hear it, all I ever think about are the moments when I felt loved, when I was in love, when I wanted to feel loved, and even when I never wanted to be loved.

In the sum of all that, I often find myself romanticizing this word — love — a lot in my life.

IN MY WORDS...

Love, like water
I think that love is like water —
necessary for living, a true supporter.
Without it, people die inside,
misunderstood, lonely, with no one to confide.
Some have an ocean, vast and deep,
never feeling its worth, they let it seep.
Some live in deserts, dry and bare,
only imagining what love feels like there.

They see mirages, chasing a dream,
Believing it's love – though not what it seems.
Heartache awaits, quietly in disguise,
A cruel illusion before their eyes.

Some have it pure, in its truest form –
a rare blessing, a shelter in a storm.
Others take whatever is near,
not seeing the damage, not feeling the fear.

Some waste it, believing it will return,
While others save it, letting their hearts burn.
They try to keep it for all their lives,
But love, like water, fades and survives.

In my opinion grief is about the love which got left behind ,
an unspoken love .
Things we wanted to say ,
gestures we could have put
to just make them understand how much we loved them ,
But now it's just too late for that ,it's time to face the worst
Nightmare

Chapter 1

Denial

MY ASSUMPTIONS

People often say I over react over small things too much,
I notice too much

I give importance to small things more than it's necessary,
I read between the lines

and assume what they meant

but if it's true then why they prove me right by the end every time

if it's true then why my assumptions often get more evidence than
the signs of their good intentions and affections

How am I supposed to react when I see the stranger in the face of my own favourite person?

How am I supposed to react when I hear the most soul shattering
words from the person I showed my deepest hurt to?

I guess I never learn or they will never understand or maybe they never meant to understand

SIGNS OF YOU

I was used to people coming,
then leaving without a sign.
I knew nothing lasts forever,
but you convinced me otherwise–
and I believed you.

Then why am I still searching
for signs of you?

IS IT REALLY OVER OR I JUST IMAGINED THE UTOPIA

I question myself was it even real,
Was it even mine,
Was he even mine ?

The loss I am feeling ,is it even mine ?
If not , then why can I still hear
the songs you sang for me ?

Why do the things you gave me
still stare deep into my soul ,
asking 'where is he?'

If it's really over then why
i still wish u would come back
and sing another song for me
till I blush until my cheek hurts .

But if it was real for you ,
you would be here with me .
Not sure for you–
but it was real for me .

LOST TWIN

You took a piece of my soul away ,
Yet i wait for you, thinking you'll stay

My eyes grow tired,but still they roam ,
Searching the sky for your way back to me

My heart can feel you drifting far ,
But I whisper–no,that's not who you are.

My arms lose slowly the warmth of you,
Yet I tell myself it cannot be true.

But you acted like it never bothered you,
You held on to your pride and defined us as past

But i can't believe that love could undo
It was real for me, it must be for you too,

I DON'T MISS YOU

I don't miss you when I feel lonely
I don't miss you when I have nobody to talk
I don't miss you when my eyes burn heavy or when I feel I'm about
to burst into tears

I miss you when I accomplish something,
I miss you when I am done being the strong girl all day,
just need to rant about bad day to 40 minutes straight

I miss you when the world gets mean
I miss you when I get spicy gossip
I miss you when i need somebody to lean
Somebody who once was always—you

Chapter - 2

Anger

"You never described a word about me
and I could never complete a sentence
without saying
your name "

" i want somebody who stays through the rain and storms not only when the sun comes up "

" how can i blame the storm for the mess it made, when it was me who opened the window"

"You came to heal the part of me
Only to tear it apart"

"The urge of human to always walk away from things they desperately want"

" You are not weak for crying , you are not dramatic for feeling like your chest might collapse under the wait of missing them --- this is the grief you are feeling .

Not just the person , but the version of you that existed with them
What's the worst part ? they are not here to hold space for the pain they created , this loneliness is excruciating "

" they didn't choose you fully ,
But that doesn't mean you're not
Worth being chosen fully "
He didn't lacked love , he lacked **capacity"**

" i gave you my heart and you only knew how to hold parts of it –
You took my laughter , my light , my softness but left my soul
waiting at the door "

YOU ARE NOT COMING BACK

I have accepted the fact that you are not coming back
You are not coming back home to me,
You are not coming back to ask how I have been,
You are not coming back to hear all the misery I have faced,

You are not coming back to see if I am still smiling like an idiot,
You are not coming back because you were not the person I
thought you were or maybe I am not somebody you can admire
anymore.

I FORGAVE YOU

I forgave you for all thing you never apologies for
I forgave you for your all the empty promises
I forgave you for taking me to the sky and then making me do the
Sky fall after that

I forgave you
for leaving me in the dark
when I just needed a hug.

Chapter - 3

Bargaining

JUST TELL ME

What should I do?
Where should I go?
Just give me magic potion to forget all that
Just tell me it was all a lie
Just tell me it was all an act
Just tell me you still care just tell me
it will be okay

'TOO MUCH'

You said I am too much,
when all I did was struggle
to Clothe put my agony into words,
That′s when I knew-
you never truly cared.

Now, I've tamed the urge
to ask you why,
To ask you 'how could you gave up on me,
on us so easily.
How you walked away without leaving a trace.

But i remind myself:
There is no sense
in holding close
The ones who chose not to stay

Was i too much ?
When i gave you
All the love i had,

When i showed you what real care feels like-
Or was i simply more
Than you could hold ?

Chapter -4

Depression

COMMON GROUND

We started off our bond
with common favourite shows,
favourite actors,
same vibes,
same attitude
and our complimentary ideologies–
but now,
what we all have in common
is that we both didn't love me.
You showed that by not staying,
and I by not leaving.

2:30 am

It all started and ended with 2:30 am
At starting, I used to burst into laughter and joy I couldn't help falling for you
And now, when the clock hits 2:30 am I often find myself falling apart questioning everything

SEPARATION AND REPLACEMENT

I think now I know
where all the love goes
when people separate their ways–
it never goes anywhere;
it just gets replaced with the latest feelings.
Insults replace the good memories,

loneliness replaces the feeling of being with them,
a tortured heart replaces the heart full of love,
tears replace the eyes brimming with affection.
And in the end,
what's left
is just our lost soul.

MULTIVERSE

Now that i am maimed
With the explosion of separation-
I often think about the things we planned
But we couldn′t do .

But As a marvel fan,
I still hope there's a universe
Where we tried the hot chocolate
From cafe bloom

I hope there's a universe where
You finally got the bike you always wanted

I hope there's a universe where
We stayed best of friends

I hope there's a universe where
I never had to wait for you endlessly

I hope there's a universe where
We had the ending like Ted and Robin
(ref: how i met your mother)

I hope there's a universe
Where you never left

I hope there's a universe
Where we never met

LOSING WHAT EXACTLY ?

I don't know how I ended up here,
we always knew we were temporary,
never meant to last–
yet it feels like I've lost everything I wished for,
like I've lost my twin,
a part of me I'll never find again.

LITTLE DID YOU KNOW

if you think you have broke me
If you think you snatched my little heart from chest ,
If you think you have left me alone
to drink up my own sorrow best,

If you think you are sole reason for pale skin recently,
Remember -
You can never break a girl
Who's first heart heart was from her father,
Because now she has a backbone of steel.

I always knew when you fall,you do down-
but when you fall for somebody who not there to catch you ,
You crash land ,after all

"You played me so well that I never saw the checkmate coming"

"I thought I was full of energy and charisma that made me feel like I can never sit still but now I know it was my mind which kept me occupied so I don't think about the mistakes I have made, the doubts that I bare"

"Funny how all my life,
The only time I have put myself first was when it came to choosing who would make the sacrifice"

WHAT STRONG-INDEPENDENT ELDER DAUGHTER DOES WHEN IS SHE ALONE ?

She sits with the demons who always whispers in her ears
that she's not good enough
Not good enough to make people proud
not good enough to make people stay.

not pretty enough that people look at her with love in their eyes
Not intelligent enough that people actually thinks she is talented
Not friendly enough to take jokes about her insecurities
Not busy enough to make her dreams come alive.

She cries oceans from her eyes before
telling a soul that she is hurt too
She always lies ,
So when she is alone ,
she just removes the mask and cries

The final act of love
I did was never contacting you again,
a silence heavier than words,
a goodbye without an end.

Chapter - 5

Acceptance

HOME

Home was never the place,
the walls,
or the area I come to sleep, eat, and stay.

I often found myself finding home in people–
not because I want them to be my home,
but because they once made me feel
safe, seen, heard, and protected.

When I feel I have found myself a home with somebody,
It means now I can be the real, unfiltered me.

I can feel fully seen–

someone to witness all of me:
the happy me, excited me,
anxious me, sad me,
even the depressed me.

That's what home means, right?
You stay because it's yours,
because joy lives there.

Home is where you can be the ugliest you
and no one will judge.

You don't have to be all glammed up.
Home is the roof that shields you
from every weathers and dangers,
holding everything you need
to survive safely.

So when I see my home in somebody,
I want that protection–
not just from storms outside
but from the deepest hurt,
the darkest thoughts

.

I can protect myself from danger,
but I want someone to protect my heart.

Yes, I expect.

Maybe I expect too much.

But how will love survive
if two people can't speak,
can't share what they need
to feel safe?

Communication is the key, right?
So where does your heart go
when I bare mine?

Where does your wisdom go
when I search for a cure
to save us?

Where does the sweet you go
when all I needed
was a simple,
"I am right here with you"?

Why do I feel like a stranger
in my own home?

How did you pack up all the love
and leave me homeless?

After all the great love and war,
I came to one truth:
you were a home for me,
but I was only a shelter for you

MIRAGE

After a very long time
I don't have any complaints for you
It feels really light,
I am finally breathing again
now that I am not carrying the weight
of the version of you
i made up in my mind

RAIN AND PUZZLE

I've learned at last–
a person's true nature
is a puzzle with no end.

Even seven years beside them
cannot reveal every shade.

People are like rain:
they rise like vapor,
light and unseen,
they gather into clouds,
gentle or heavy,
and fall upon us
as sudden storms or tender drops.

Then, without warning,
they vanish again,
only to return
in another form.

So I remind myself–
do not mistake people
for permanence.

Cherish the moments,
but do not love blindly.

Keep your eyes open
for the bright bows that follow,
and for the quiet truth
hidden in the changing sky.

THE IMPORTANCE OF LIVING IN THE PRESENT

You never know when a moment will be the last–
the last time you talk, the last time you meet.
So speak your truth,
show kindness
and treat others with the respect they deserve.

Because when the moment passes,
words left unsaid weigh heavy.
I know this too well–
there were so many things I wish I could have told my father,
but now I never can.

And it hurts that my final memory with him
Is not of love,
but of me as the angry elder daughter

DONE AND DUSTED

Now that we are all done and dusted,
I wish you nothing less than the best .

I hope it will remind you of me
when you'll see a flower of lily

I hope it will reminds you of me
when you will see taylor Swift

I hope it will remind you of me
When you will start another sitcom

I hope you will remember my aggressive obsession with coffee
And all the times i mispronounced every Urdu words,

I hope you will remember the good ,silly and happy me
not the sad and depressed me

Because I will always remember you , All of you .

"Your ex situationship /relationship was not
the love of your life, you just have attachment issues"

"Only if somebody was nice to you
doesn't mean that they are the most special, it's was you and
your love that made them special"

“Maybe happily ever after means ,
you moving on “

"If a relationship is making you question your worth, it's time to walk away"

"The next time you fall in love,
Just make sure that you fall in love with yourself first"

ONE TRUE LOVE

For the first time in my life,
I'm not waiting for somebody to show up for me

I'm not waiting for somebody
to hear what I had to say

I'm not waiting for somebody
to give the reassurance I deserve

I'm not waiting for somebody
to hold on to me

I'm not waiting for somebody
to surprise me with my favourite flowers

Not because I gave up,
it's because I realised that it was me,
all along I was waiting for me. myself to choose me
over anything and everything.

I was waiting for me
to notice, hear, trust
and most importantly choose myself
There was nobody, only me holding myself up each time
when storms came,

I was searching for love till the time
I realised
I was the love

WHEN LOVE FINDS ME AGAIN

I hope when love finds me again ,
It feels safe ,
It feels warmth like a fireplace
not fire crackers .

I hope when love finds me again
It brings calm to my heart not chaos

I hope when love finds me again
t feels like a warm hug not like i'm being struck by the lightning

I hope when love finds me again
I will not constantly question everything or get called crazy for
asking for reassurance

I hope when love finds me again
It won't make me question or pretend
Not 'am i too much?' Am I asking too high?
But a love that holds me tight.

I hope when love finds me again
It comes to stay for life not for a while

Love that ends , still matters because grief is just a proof that is was real and sometimes beauty is the journey not destination

Now because of some reasons
I have understood what LA LA LAND movie was all about

Final chapter

Sunshine

Sunshine is the golden touch of the sky,
warming the earth and waking life around.
It makes flowers bloom, trees whisper, and hearts glow.
With every ray, it carries hope, joy, and a promise of new beginnings.
A gentle reminder that light always follows the dark.

Same happens in our lives too ,
Light always follows the dark
And sometimes it's the people, you are surrounded by
You just need to be brave enough to wait till the dark goes and light comes up and never give up

In my case i am the lucky one for being supported by the people who pulled me every time when the darkness came in
So Final chapter is a dedicated to them,
To My sunshines.

TO MY FIRST READER

To my first reader ,
To my first friend
To my first best friend
To my first child
To my first favourite person
To my first follower

My title sister 'Tamanna '
You are my sunshine
You are my first love, the purest kind

You never left ,
You held me tight
Through every storm
Through every night

You are the me i dream to be
Patient , strong ,so full of grace
Strategic mind , a steady heart

At the very beginning,
God gifted me you
So i could never complaint
The pure love ,my soulmate

I love the fact that you have no choice but to stuck with me forever
like yin-yang , we fit just right

Thank you for being my first reader for my first book and motivating
me into completing this
Thank you for everything you have ever doing for me
Thank you for being my sunshine in the dark times
i love you the most

THE RETRIEVERS

According to the dictionary ,
Retrieve means to get and bring back
Luckily in my life , 2 retrievers came in

They brought me back to myself ,
To a version i never knew,
A version alive
A version true,

With wagging tails and endless love,
They retriever joy out of me
Made me whole again.

They showed me emotions i never thought i had,
They taught me that love needs no
Word-
Only actions,
Only presence.

Coco and Rio , my sunshines ,
My heart 's purest delight
Unconditional , boundless,
The greatest love of all.

I love you both
My retrievers,
My forever light

THE STRONGEST WARRIOR

I always knew,
No matter what comes,
I will never give up .

Even if i sink deep in mud ,
I will rise,
I will stand strong.

Because i was raised
By a warrior –
The woman i look up to ,
My mother.

She gave me everything ,
Worked all her life
To build the world I needed.

At my age,
She was already carrying us ,
Fighting battles alone ,
Yet always ahead of me ,
Shield in hand
Ready to protect.

So when life tests me ,
I think of her
And whisper to myself–
If she never gave up ,
How could i?

I never had a man
To protect and provide
But i had her –
And she is more of a MAN
Than any man could ever be .
Thank you for being my sunshine
I love you

THE BEST FRIEND

To my best friend,Yashita
My sister from another mother,
My soul-twin

I never thought i'd be so lucky
To find another sister in you .

We are the same person
In different fonts,
Living the same lives,
Thinking the same thoughts,
Agreeing on the same truths .

I'm forever grateful
That you chose me,
To be not just a friend,
But family .

'Best friend' feels too small word
For what you mean to me

In the world where ,
people come together just for the sake of
Instagram grid ,
I have found you –
A mate to share my pain,
My joy , my silliness
My doubts ,
My whole heart.

You showed me it's okay
To not be okay,
That being "too much" is a gift
Something to embrace .

With you ,
I can face anything ,
Everything

Thank you for being my sunshine
I love you always

A special thanks to my therapist Dr Shivam
for being my light and guide through hard times ,
for understanding me
when i didn't knew how to put my agony into words ,
For making me feel safe and whole again

If any of my readers are going through a hard time in their lives i would highly recommend you to ask for help and please take therapy ,
It is okay to ask for help than giving up on your own happiness

And if you ever need a friend to talk –
I am just a text away.

Thank you for reading my book , sunshine

-THE END-

Printed at Repro India Ltd.